DANIKA's
DANCING
DAY

ONCE UPON A
Dance

ILLUSTRATED BY SUDIPTA STEVE DASGUPTA

Dedicated to all those with a dancing soul.

DANIKA'S DANCING DAY
A DANCE-IT-OUT CREATIVE MOVEMENT STORY FOR YOUNG MOVERS

© 2022 ONCE UPON A DANCE Redmond, WA
Illustrated by Sudipta Steve Dasgupta, www.dasguptarts.com

Each Dance-It-Out! story is an independent kids' dance performance ready for the imagination stage.
This book builds on previous material and is best for dance students or as a sequel to other *Dance-It-Out!* stories.
Danika's a little girl with a dancing heart and soul who brings ballet into her every-day life, including her chores and naps.
Ballerina Konora joins each page to help readers connect with movement, learn ballet, and explore dance fundamentals.

Library of Congress Control Number: 2021925198
ISBN 978-1-955555-14-2 (ebook); 978-1-955555-13-5 (paperback); 978-1-955555-15-9 (hardcover)
Juvenile Fiction: Performing Arts / Dance; (Juvenile Fiction: Imagination & Play)
(Juvenile Fiction: Interactive Adventures; Juvenile Fiction: Animals: Squirrels)
First Edition

Other ONCE UPON A DANCE Titles:
Joey Finds His Jump!: A Dance-It-Out Creative Movement Story for Young Movers
Petunia Perks Up: A Dance-It-Out Movement and Meditation Story
Dayana, Dax, and the Dancing Dragon: A Dance-It-Out Creative Movement Story for Young Movers
Danny, Denny, and the Dancing Dragon: A Dance-It-Out Creative Movement Story for Young Movers
Princess Naomi Helps a Unicorn: A Dance-It-Out Creative Movement Story for Young Movers
The Cat with the Crooked Tail: A Dance-It-Out Creative Movement Story for Young Movers
Brielle's Birthday Ball: A Dance-It-Out Creative Movement Story for Young Movers
Mira Monkey's Magic Mirror Adventure: A Dance-It-Out Creative Movement Story for Young Movers
Belluna's Adventure in the Sky: A Dance-It-Out Creative Movement Story for Young Movers
Freya, Fynn, and the Fantastic Flute: A Dance-It-Out Creative Movement Story for Young Movers
Sadoni Squirrel: Superhero: A Dance-It-Out Creative Movement Story for Young Movers
Andi's Valentine Tree: A Dance-It-Out Creative Movement Story for Young Movers
Dancing Shapes: Ballet and Body Awareness for Young Dancers
More Dancing Shapes: Ballet and Body Awareness for Young Dancers
Nutcracker Dancing Shapes: Shapes and Stories from Konora's Twenty-Five Nutcracker Roles
Dancing Shapes with Attitude: Ballet and Body Awareness for Young Dancers
Konora's Shapes: Poses from Dancing Shapes for Creative Movement & Ballet Teachers
More Konora's Shapes: Poses from More Dancing Shapes for Creative Movement & Ballet Teachers
Ballerina Dreams Ballet Inspiration Journal/Notebook
Dancing Shapes Ballet Inspiration Journal/Notebook

Hello Fellow Dancer,

My name is Ballerina Konora. I love stories, adventures, and ballet.

I'm glad you're here with me! Will you be my dance partner and tell the story along with Danika and me? I've included descriptions of movements that express the story. You can decide whether to use these ideas, the illustrations, or create your own moves.

Be safe, of course, and do what works for your body in your space. And if you'd rather just settle in and enjoy the pictures, that's fine, too.

Konora

P.S. You don't have to be a cat to act like Penelope. Anyone can dance like all the characters and creatures in this story.

ONCE UPON A DANCE, Danika opened her eyes, clapped her hands in excitement, and bounced out of bed. It was time to begin her dancing day. Danika was a budding ballerina, and each dawn offered the chance for a new performance. The sunrise was Danika's cue that the stage curtain would open soon.

And she couldn't wait!

Time for ballet practice. Today's story has a lot of dance terms. All of the dance terms are in italics, and the words in blue appear in the glossary at the back.

Danika woke up feeling excited. Here's what I do when I'm super-excited: I clap my hands together and rub them back and forth really fast. Will you try it with me?

Next, let's re-create Danika's stretch in the picture. Stretch your arms up in a V, like you're pushing the corners of the room away, and give a little yawn.

Danika was in a hurry to complete her chores so she could focus on the day's performance. She smiled, thinking how happy her mother would be to see the kitchen clean and sparkling.

Danika pretended she was warming up in preparation for her show. She *pliéd* up and down while she scrubbed the walls and cupboards. Then she used her feet as a *tendu* mop. As her toes moved across the floor, the tiles began to shine.

Imagine we're happy Danika doing our chores. Let's do *pliés* in *first position,* toes out to the side and heels facing in. Bend your knees out to the side. Go up and down as you scrub the walls. Keep your back upright and imagine you have a glass of water on your head you're trying not to spill.

We can *tendu* front, side, and back. Try to keep your legs straight by standing up tall as you start and finish your *tendu.*

The *tendus* left Danika's socks covered in dust. She wiped them off with a *sur le cou-de-pied*, which was also a good way to get her feet ready for her performance.

Let's get that dust off the bottoms of our feet. Put one heel up and rest it on the other ankle. Wrap your toes around to the back to do the ballet move. Pretend you have an itch on the bottom of your foot and move your whole foot up and down. If that seems difficult, practice balancing on one foot any way you like. Or try to do it while you hold on to something.

Oh no! Now we have dirt all over our legs—perhaps this isn't really the best way to clean our socks after all?

As she moved the chairs to clean under the table, Danika imagined she was a choreographer placing famous ballerinas in position for the opening number. Act 1 was about to begin. In her mind, the room was already full of dancers standing on the chairs, and the curtain was about to open!

First, lean over to move the chair. Let's imagine we're one of twenty-four dancers waiting for the curtain to open. What is your pose? Dancers work hard to keep their places, spacing, and movements synchronized, meaning they move together at the same time. In my imagination, the dancers have ribbons, which they swirl in circles. Perhaps grab a real scarf or ribbon for extra fun?

Danika pulled out her dancing partner for the morning: the vacuum cleaner.

Vacuuming was one of her favorite chores. She glided and *waltzed* around the room and pretended she was part of a big group dance at a fancy ball. Danika pictured a beautiful stage where dancers in matching outfits *waltzed* in a dizzying whirlpool of colors.

Have you heard of Cinderella? She's a make-believe dancing princess. Let's pretend we're Cinderella at the ball, dancing around a decorated room with the music powering us forward. To start the *waltz*, brush one foot forward, then take three tiptoe steps, turn halfway around and brush your other leg backward. We're light on our feet, as if we are dancing on an enormous cake, skating around on the frosting.

Danika's partner held her steady as she performed *arabesques* and *penchés* in a glorious outfit with a fanciful tiara on top of her head.

Find something sturdy to help you balance and send one leg up behind you. Reach your toes far away, but try to keep your hips as still as possible. To *penché*, I pretend I'm a teapot tipping my tea out while holding my same teapot shape.

Danika finished her chores, but wasn't ready to stop dancing. She wanted to share her happiness with the sky and the trees. She *chasséd* out the door and headed to the garden.

Act 2 was about to begin.

Can you gallop around like a horse? Imagine that one foot likes to stay in front the whole time, and it sneaks out just when the other leg catches up. Bend your knees as you stretch a foot forward and step onto it. Straighten both legs as you scoop them together in a small jump. Keep moving forward with each step and jump.

Danika skipped around her favorite tree. "Your leaves look very handsome today," she told the tree as she moved faster and faster around its trunk. When she finally stopped, her eyes fell upon the perfect stage for her next move.

Danika hurried over to the sidewalk and began to perform *sauté arabesques*. With each step, she imagined the rabbits and squirrels were watching her, spellbound by her dance.

Skipping is so much fun. Put one leg in *passé* with your knee facing front. Hop in the air. Then step forward and hop on the other leg. Keep stepping and switching. It's like a jumping march with a happy little scooch.

Let's do that *arabesque* again, but this time, add a little hop. *Sauté arabesque* is a lot like skipping, except our leg goes behind us. These moves can take some practice to figure out, so go slowly at first.

The neighbor's little cat, Penelope, reminded her of another jump she enjoyed, *pas de chat*, which translates to "step of the cat" in French, the language the ballet words come from. Danika performed the tricky step for Penelope.

For *pas de chat*, start with one leg in *passé*. Your toes touch the other leg, and your two legs make a triangle. Then, as if jumping over something sideways, reach your bent leg out, jump, and end up in the same position on the other leg. It will take some practice to get it all into one movement. Try it in slow motion at first.

Suddenly, the grass and trees surrounding Danika rose as if they were dancers, ready to join her ballet. The swaying of the grass reminded her of *port de bras* (in French, it means carrying the arms), and she circled her arms in the wind. The trees were her backup dancers, creating *attitudes* with their bent branches.

Float your arms as if the wind is gently carrying them. Circle with your arms around, then try other shapes.

To create an *attitude*, do another *passé*, our position from the previous page. Then lift your knee higher so your leg ends up halfway between a kick and a *passé*. You can make *attitudes* to the front, side, or back.

The beautiful sun inspired Danika to make round shapes with her arms in *first*, *second*, and *fifth positions*. Her happiness overflowed into a little twirl. She imagined she was center stage, with dancers circling around her like planets orbiting the sun.

Pretend to hold a big balloon in front of your chest. That's called *first position* (arms). Now, keep the arm shape, but lift your arms up almost above your head. Keep them a little in front of you with your back straight. Now your arms are in *fifth position*. Next, return to first, then expand your balloon as far as it will go without popping, with your hands lower than your shoulders. With your arms in this shape, you are in *second position*.

Dancing made Danika happy, but it also made her a little sleepy. She twirled offstage and sank down to the ground. With a big yawn, she curled up for nap backstage in the shade of her favorite tree. The minute Danika was on the ground, Penelope the cat snuggled up next to her.

Enjoy spinning however you like—just watch out for furniture and pets. As you spin to the floor, first bend your knees to get lower, touch the floor with one hand, then put one knee down just before rolling onto your bottom.

Next up is napping! Aren't naps the best? Curl up and relax your muscles. Imagine the warmth of kitty fur on your arm. This feeling makes me want to wriggle with happiness.

But even as Danika drifted off to sleep, her ballet was not finished. The dramatic third act was just beginning.

She continued her dance in her dreams. The birds in the tree joined her in a stunning dream choreography. An audience of rabbits and squirrels tapped the rhythm with their tails and toes. As the dream *ensemble* performed, the sky created a beautiful cloud-filled backdrop.

Show me how you like to dance. Make up your own movements? Imagine the birds are your partners. Perhaps you want to put a little music on?

I feel happy when I act like the rabbits and squirrels, having a good time tapping my toes, and swishing my tail.

And because this was the best kind of dream, anything could happen. For the finale, Danika flew with the birds as she *grand jetéd.* She leaped high into the sky, as if carried by the wind.

To perform a *grand jeté,* reach one leg out in front of you with your bent knee over your toes. Jump over a puddle in your imagination. Land on one foot with your knee over your toes and your leg behind you.

Danika twirls through life, making even the most ordinary experiences remarkable. Each day offers the excitement of finding her next dance inspiration. What inspires you?

The audience thunderously applauded. The curtain closed.

Thee end! The end.

(My grandfather always ended stories this way,
and I like to share the fun.)

Thank you for being my dance partner.

Love,

Konora

Fancy French

Plié ['plee-AY'] bend (bent/bending)

Tendu ['tawn-DOO'] stretched
(might also hear *battement tendu*)

Sur le Cou-de-Pied ['sur-leh-koo-deh-pee-AY'] on the neck of the foot

Arabesque ['air-a-BESK'] a decorative pattern of intertwined flowing lines

Penché [pawn-SHAY'] leaning

Chassé ['sha-SAY'] chased

Passé ['pah-SAY'] passed
(*passé* is the movement, *retiré* is the position, both words are used)

Sauté ['so-TAY'] jumped (jumps/jumping)

Pas de Chat ['pah-deh-SHAW'] step of the cat

Port de Bras ['pore-deh-BRA'] carriage of the arms

Ensemble ['On-som-bull'] from the French word *ensemblée*: together (a group of dancers)

Grand Jeté ['grawn zhuh-TAY'] big throw

Sous Sus ['su-su'] over-under (or under the above) (might also see *sous sous* or *sus sous*)
(*Sous sus* most often refers to the movement getting into the position.)

Other Dance Terms

First Position (feet) heels face each other, toes out to the side
(One way to find first is to rock back onto the heels and open the toes to the side as much as possible, then drop the toes down in a V.)

Waltz a turning dance step that goes down-up-down
(Really, more like down-up-up-up. Waltz is a German word meaning to roll or revolve.)
(In this story, we learned half of a ballet waltz.)

Skip (Sauté Passé) stepping from one foot to the other with a hop or bounce

Attitude the working leg lifts in the air in a bent position to the front, side, or back

First Position (arms) round arms held in front, between the chest and belly button

Second Position (arms) arms to the side, slightly in front and below the shoulders

Fifth Position (arms) rounded arms above the head, slightly in front

Twirl turning, usually on tiptoes
For a challenge, try twirling in a *sous sus* position (pictured)

Choreographer a person who creates dances

Synchronized moving together, occurring at the same time or rate

If you're looking for music inspiration, check out our Spotify Playlists:
OnceUponADance
- Dramatic Chill Dancing
- Energetic Dance Music
- Favorite Ballet Music

We'd Love to Connect!

We are a mother-daughter pair who were both happily immersed in the ballet world until March 2020. We hope by the time you read this, life is on its way back to normal, and we can all have dance parties with our friends again.

In the meantime, we check for reviews daily, and we'd be immensely grateful for a kind, honest review on Amazon or Goodreads or a shout-out or follow on social media if you enjoy our books.

www.OnceUponADance.com
www.CreativeMovementStories.com
@Once_UponADance (Instagram)
OnceUponADanceViralDancing (Facebook)

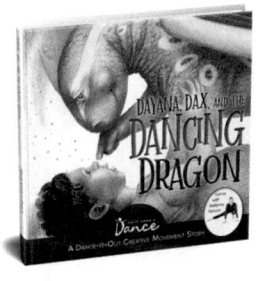

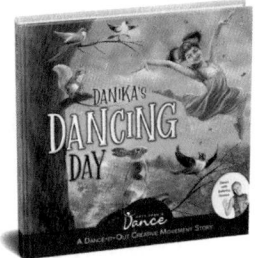

Made in the USA
Monee, IL
07 November 2022

17249711R00024